M000208708

HEROES OF PLANET EARTH
Black Hole

HOPE: Heroes of Planet Earth – Black Hole

Copyright © 2023. All rights reserved to Sole Books an imprint of Wild Soccer USA.

This is a work of fiction. Names, characters, places, and incidents are either products of the author's imagination or used fictitiously. Any resemblance to actual events, locales, or persons, living or dead, is entirely coincidental. No part of this book may be reproduced, stored in a retrieval system, or transmitted in any form or by any means, electronic, mechanical, photocopying, recording, or otherwise, without prior written permission from the publisher. For permission requests, contact: Sole Books, P.O. Box 10445, Beverly Hills, CA 90213. Unauthorized use, reproduction, or distribution of the ™ HOPE: Heroes of Planet Earth logo and title without the express written permission of Sole Books is strictly prohibited. For more information and permission request contact Sole Books, P.O. Box 10445, Beverly Hills CA 90213

Series created and cowritten by Y Ginsberg
Editor: Yaron Ginsberg
Cover design: Mirko Pohle
Cover Illustration: Guy Lenman
Inside pages design: Lazar Kackarovski

Library of Congress Cataloging-in-Publication data available.

Print ISBN: 978-1938591-95-2
eBook ISBN: 978-1-938591-41-9

Published by Sole Books, an imprint of Wild Soccer USA, Beverly Hills, California. Printed in the United States of America. First printing June 2023.
First edition.

www.solebooks.com

HEROES

OF

PLANET EARTH

Black Hole

MICHAEL PART

Sole
BOOKS

CHAPTER 1

The whole thing started when Martin "Marty" Mayhew was forced to live on the oil rig known as *the Black Hole*, by his billionaire stepfather who owned it and believed he also owned Marty.

Marty floated on his board, a 5'8" Wetworks Thruster shaped by Jacca Seco from Brazil, next to a tangle of corner steel. It was not every day a fifteen-year-old boy got to surf a quick, almost-perfect wave off the side of an oil rig. He looked up at the star-filled nighttime sky. The platform rig was ten stories high and lit up like a Houston used car lot, something he was familiar with having lived for the last five years in the Lone Star State.

He listened to the sea. He considered himself an expert in *ocean listening*. After all, he had spent most of his life surfing growing up in La Jolla, California. But then, one day, his mother married Horace Clearwater, the oil magnet and owner of United Petroleum. They moved to Texas, and he had to leave behind the things he loved most.

You spend a lot of time in the water, you hear things, he thought. There was a sound the ocean made for many different things and there was one the South Atlantic Ocean made, when it made a wave. Waves came in sets of threes or fours or tens or what-have-you, depending on the break and one was due here. He knew it was due because he *heard* it. The last set he had just missed rolled in five minutes ago. Three waves, twelve seconds apart, the third being the tallest and the one to catch.

He needed one quick enough to escape. That's all that counted now because there was no talking his way out of this one. His stepbrother's men were definitely after him and he knew it would only be a matter of heartbeats before they showed up, gunning for him.

How did it get so bad? Everything was chill —sort of. But then I had to take an evening stroll. I couldn't just close my eyes and go to sleep like a good little boy, I had to wander around the rig. And see what I wasn't supposed to see.

The night started out warm and humid. There was a slight breeze coming off the continent, blowing foam off the tops of the waves that formed off the starboard side of the rig, smelling like mangos and flowers. The lights on the rig reflected off the water and a fleet of pelicans soared over the nearby reef, fishing. Toward the center of the rig, where the base pipe with the well-head turned twenty-four hours a day, oil sucked from the bottom of the sea. Yellow light chevrons panned up and down, back and forth. Marty moved in closer for a better look. He gasped.

He saw his stepbrother, Simon, and two of his men turning the valves, releasing the crude from the drill, not into the tank, but right into the deep blue sea. They were spilling oil – on purpose.

That didn't make any sense. Why would they do it? United Petroleum made billions off this oil. Marty hated them for that but spilling the oil into the ocean was much worse.

He couldn't hold back. Could he? Then again, he did that a lot. Shoot his mouth off. *"Do you ever think before you speak?"* More than one teacher has said to him. They told him he was lazy. *Yeah, maybe I'm lazy*, he thought. Lazy when it came to doing the boring things everyone else around him did. And they didn't know anything about him and that was fine because he knew it would upset them to know what he was really interested in. It would upset them because he hated everything that was dear to them.

At this point, he stopped wondering why his stepfather had sent him to the oil rig. Did the old man know that Marty was passionate about protecting the environment, especially marine life? The irony of sending him to an oil rig was a cruel joke, the kind of joke that a ruthless, cynical stepfather would make.

But being on the rig wasn't that bad. He surfed a lot. Secretly, he was filming videos about life on the rig, which he planned to use later.

But now he was watching a channel he couldn't turn off. Something horrible.

"What are you doing?" he yelled at them.

Startled, Simon jerked his head up and saw Marty standing four stories above him on the top of the rig, watching them spill oil into the ocean. For Marty, this meant death to all sea creatures, plants, and birds for many miles around. For Simon, it meant he was caught and his goody-two-shoes stepbrother saw everything. He flashed Marty a smile, and Marty knew what it meant.

"Get him! Now!" Simon barked at his men.

Marty ducked and ran with all his might when they gave chase. He had less than a minute to get it done. Two of Simon's men charged up the stairs, so he went down, passing his cabin, seeing his comfortable bed one last time. He went to the infirmary and threw open a stainless-steel drawer labeled RFID. He grabbed the white injector and loaded it. He took the chip label, shoved it in his pocket, and swabbed his hand with iodine. Forty-five seconds. Then he quickly slammed the needle just below the surface between his thumb and forefinger and pushed the plunger. The chip slid in, and he yanked the injector out and tossed it back in the drawer. Fifteen seconds. He closed the drawer, tiptoed to the door, checked in both directions, then ran back to his quarters. He grabbed his surfboard, dove off the rig's starboard side just ahead of Simon's men, and plummeted fifty feet down, splashing into the dark waters below the rig. His minute was up.

He heard a familiar noise and his heart pounded out of his chest. There was no doubt how bad it had gotten. They were coming for him.

The menacing approach of the boats was dim at first but grew louder quickly. In seconds, the sound of their engines drowned out all else. Three of them. He tried not to panic. He flattened out on his board and paddled like crazy. It was his only chance. He came around the rear corner of the Black Hole and paddled to where he knew the wave would peak, the take-off point, just as the first roller rose up next to the rig.

He cranked around so he faced the wave. The ten-foot bump lifted him up as it raced toward the distant shore and when he was at the highest point, he could see the second wave already forming behind it.

That's when three Zodiac rafts with powerful Mercury outboard motors screamed from behind the oil rig, carrying two men apiece, each aiming an AK-47 in his direction.

Marty's eyes widened as bursts of fire flashed from the distant gun barrels. The rafts drew closer. He quickly duck-dived under the passing wave as rounds jetted into the water like angry hummingbirds all around him, missing him. He had to get that third wave, so he waited as the second wave lifted him up. As it passed, it made him more visible to the approaching rafts.

A third wave formed behind him. It was a giant 12-foot wave that swallowed him whole. He spun his board around and paddled furiously as the wave built up beneath him. When he glanced back, it looked like someone had stood up in bed under blue covers.

And attacked.

7.62 millimeter rounds poked the wall of water all around him as he pushed his board down, catching the wave, popping up.

A sudden offshore breeze blew the foam off the curling lip and blasted painful droplets in Marty's face as he reached the bottom.

The Zodiacs crested the back of the wave, all guns blazing.

Marty cranked the board right and crouched as the wave curled over him, locking him into a head-high tube, disappearing inside just as the Zodiacs tumbled down the face of the giant wave, slamming into each other as they plunged to the bottom, knocking a couple guys out.

Marty ducked and the tube closed him into a chamber, a small, enclosed area of water created by a wave breaking over a reef. He heard the hollow echo *bloop* of the air sucking out and a split second later he was spit out at the other end, drenched in a fine salty mist.

He smiled. Then he saw his pursuers, who were waiting for him at the other end. Knowing he was sunk, Marty reached for the sky.

They got him. The Zodiacs – all three of them - were waiting for him. The giant of a man in the lead boat wore a black leather coat, and leveled his weapon at Marty. He was a burly kind of guy with a blonde beard and crooked fangs. He was new to the rig and went by the name of Giddings.

"Your brother is expecting you," he said calmly. Marty noted his accent had a hint of Irish, so faint, he'd almost missed it.

"Tell him I'm not in," Marty quipped as Giddings reached over and grabbed Marty by the scruff of his neck and yanked him into the Zodiac, leaving his board behind. "We insist."

"My board!" Marty yelled. The pain in his neck was excruciating but it wasn't as bad as leaving his board behind.

"What are you worried about?" Giddings asked. "Now you'll always know where to find it." Then he chuckled. Giddings started the outboard motor, nodded to his men in the other crafts to follow him as he motored away. Marty was watching desperately as his board disappeared behind a swell, his only means of escape gone. He kept watching it bob in the sea like a potato chip, drifting slowly on a rip current that quickly pulled it over the nearby reef.

CHAPTER 2

Giddings steered the Zodiac into its berth against the wooden platform at the bottom of the rig and one of his men tied it off.

"Home sweet home, huh?" Marty quipped.

Giddings scowled. "Not for much longer eh," he grinned. He grabbed Marty, lifted him up over his head, and tossed him like a ragdoll onto the steel platform. "More like your last stop," he sneered.

Marty tried to roll away, but Giddings jumped out of the raft and kicked him, slamming him against the far bulkhead.

He got up on one elbow but stayed down. He hurt all over. He wished he'd never set foot on the Black Hole.

Giddings reached down and picked him up by the back of his shirt with one hand and set him down on the steel staircase leading up. "Walk," the giant said and jammed his pistol into Marty's back.

"Glock 43X," Marty said, as he went up the stairs, identifying the gun that was poking him in the back.

Giddings wasn't impressed. He gave him a shove and grabbed Marty around the neck with meaty fingers, squeezing off his oxygen.

Marty's face turned red as he held off his defense. He knew how to move against the big goon who took pleasure in hurting him, but also knew it was too soon to act. Giddings waited and just before he thought Marty was about to lose consciousness, he let go, leaving a purple vanishing handprint on the boy's neck. "Move it," he said and shoved Marty ahead of him.

Marty climbed the stairs, rubbing his neck, gulping down air. "I'm fine, by the way," he said, finally reaching the top of the stairs.

"Oh, too bad," Giddings said, throwing open the Level 7 door and shoving Marty inside, where he tripped over the knee-knocker that kept the water out in stormy weather, sprawling on the oil-slick linoleum-on-steel floor, face first. *This was a waterless storm*, he thought. He raised his head and looked around. It was his stepbrother Simon's quarters and office.

Simon was behind his sun-bleached teak desk and stood when Marty flew in. He was well built, in his 30s, tough, like a prizefighter. He was tall like his father, Horace, and had long black hair slicked back. He gave Marty a gaze, identified as his dead-eyed wolfish look. He had a tiny scar above his left eyebrow, and he sported a bunch of gold earrings.

Marty struggled to get to his feet. No one helped. "Don't be mad at him, brother, he's new, right? Besides, I think I started it."

"Shut-up while you're ahead, Marty," Simon said.

"Am I?" Marty asked.

"Are you what-?"

"Ahead," Marty replied.

Simon sighed. "What am I going to do with you?"

"I guess a medal for stopping an ecological disaster is out of the question?" Marty replied.

Simon narrowed his eyes. "Good guess."

"Dad knows what you're up to?"

Simon nodded to Giddings, who clubbed Marty across the side of his head with a giant slap that sent him clanging into a grimy locker mounted in the wall.

"He's not your dad," Simon said. "He's *my* dad."

The pain was excruciating. Marty thought that Simon was right. He had a real father. But Marty's father was long dead. He felt the pain building in his stomach but didn't let it grow. He had to act fast. "You think dad would be okay knowing your goons shot real bullets out there?" Marty asked, rubbing the side of his head. "I could have gotten hurt."

Simon smiled cruelly. "You'll never learn, Marty. Horace sent you here for a reason. If my men had wanted to hit you, they would have."

"So, help me do my homework bro," Marty said.

Simon studied his stepbrother. "The lesson is there's always one in every family. You know the type – the one that bites the hand that feeds him." He nodded to Giddings. "Get him outta here."

"What should I do with him?"

"Lock him up."

Giddings seized Marty and dragged him away. He opened an empty cabin at the end of the corridor and pushed him inside.

"Come on, man, I need my phone!" Marty said. "It's in my cabin."

Giddings let out a really nasty, wicked laugh.

"I don't think so," he said.

He slammed the door tight.

Marty waited until Giddings' footsteps died away, then he fished his waterproof smartphone from his vest pocket. He opened the RFID app he had coded the previous month and activated the chip in his hand. It still hurt. He didn't have time to do a good job of it, but at least it had stopped bleeding. At least it worked.

He waited a few seconds for the person on the other end to receive the data. When he got the ack, her name and face flashed on his screen. He grinned. Gabby Ferrari's profile picture had a mischievous gaze, but deep down she was fearless and relentless.

He had met Gabby at an international climate rally in Austin last summer and they had stayed in touch ever since. Gabby was a very vocal and globally known climate activist, who wasn't very popular nowadays with a lot of people. Her life was regularly in danger, so she had to move from one place to another quite often. She had a network of loyal friends who were ready to help her at will and Marty was one of them. But now it was he who needed her help.

He gave her a beta copy of his app so no one could hack their chats. He knew he could trust her to do the right thing. She told him she would make a surprise appearance at a *Save the Rainforest* summit in Sao Paulo, and he told her he'd love to meet her there later in the week. But now he needed her help. She was just an hour's flight away from the rig. He knew he could trust her to do the right thing.

Hi Gabby, I figure you're not far away. I discovered an intentional oil spill at United Petroleum's Black Hole oil rig. They locked me up. I might be in danger. Marty.

He added the coordinates of the Black Hole and dialed Gabby's number. His message should have landed on her phone in exactly four seconds.

He felt a bit better after he punched the 'send' button. Relieved, he slumped to the cold floor, his jaw still throbbing. He was exhausted, but he couldn't relax. He kept wondering what would happen next.

He knew that Simon would soon conclude that he had to silence him, and he wondered why he hadn't done it already. Maybe he had to report back to Horace. Get a green light before he could murder his stepbrother.

I have to get out of here fast, he thought.

And before that thought was halfway over, he fell asleep.

He woke up with a start from a terrible nightmare and looked at his watch. He had been locked up for twenty-four hours. *OMG*. He checked his phone but there was no reply. He wondered why Gabby hadn't responded. He was hungry. Then he remembered: That morning, they had given him very little to eat. French fries and a tuna sandwich with a bottle of coke. He suspected they put something in the coke that made him sleepy. He did some stretches to clear his head.

Not long after that, Giddings stormed in.

"Show time!" he announced. "Let's go."

He shoved Marty out the door, holding him tightly. They made their way to the central area of the platform. The deafening roar of the rotating wellhead filled the air. In the middle stood a tall tower-like structure, with a drilling rig at its center. The rig had a long pipe attached to it, extending from the top of the platform all the way down into the ocean. The pipe which usually penetrated through rocks on the ocean floor was hanging on the water surface, creating a turbulent whirlpool approximately fifty feet below. Its three sharp steel blades spun rapidly, churning the water into a frenzy.

Giddings shoved Marty to the edge. Marty looked down and had one thought. He wondered how long he could hold his breath. Simon stepped out of the shadows, revealing himself.

"Are you out of your mind?!" Marty shouted at him.

Simon smiled. "I don't think father would be upset hearing about what happened," he said, sounding like a prosecutor presenting his case. "You jammed the well-head in the base pipe, causing a spill. However, while trying to grab onto the base-pipe to prevent your fall, you slipped and slid all the way down the shaft to sea level, where the well-head caught your shirt and dragged you under. By the time we could stop the drill, you had already been torn to pieces.'"

"Nice touch, you lying jerk," Marty said and sucked in a breath. He looked at his hands. They were shaking. He twisted out of Giddings' grip, turned to run, and slammed into Simon's chest. Giddings grabbed him instantly and held him fast.

He tried to maintain his composure, but a sense of dread washed over him. "It won't work. Dad isn't going to believe you," he muttered through his clenched teeth.

"Why do you care, you aren't going to witness how my plan will pan out," Simon said with a cruel smile.

Marty's heart was racing. For the first time in his life, he was truly terrified. He had to come up with something, but with what?

Giddings was ready. He enjoyed the moment and his eyes flashed in anticipation.

So, this is what evil looks like, Marty thought.

There was no more waiting. He had to move. Fast.

CHAPTER 3

Giddings definitely asked for it, Marty thought.

The giant's huge hands came towards him, ready to push him over the edge and into the abyss. But Marty was ready for him. He clenched his free hand into a fist and slammed it into Giddings' crotch. Part A in a self–defense move he perfected that earned him his third–degree Black Belt in *American Tang Soo Do* last year.

Giddings let out a high-pitched scream, which was common when this maneuver was inflicted on an enemy. Marty's swift hit took him by surprise.

Marty thanked in his heart his martial arts teachers for everything they had taught him. Giddings couldn't thank anyone because, engulfed in pain, he let go of his prey and uselessly buckled over. Marty completed his move by grabbing Giddings by his hair and yanking him onto his back. The giant of a man landed with a thud and skidded headfirst over the slippery precipice, plunging fifty feet into the sea. Marty could hear Giddings's screams as he tumbled through the air, smashing into the base pipe. He then crumpled, falling into the sea like a rag doll.

Seconds later, he sank, disappearing into the inky blackness.

Simon drew his pistol and spun to Marty. Marty kicked the gun out of his hand and leaped into the abyss after Giddings. He streaked downward, hitting the water and swimming furiously away from the turning drill rig. After a couple of quick strokes, he grabbed a nearby ladder rung to keep from getting sucked into the vortex of the whirlpool the drill created. He looked down and saw Giddings fighting for his life. He grabbed a rope and tied it to the ladder. He then threw it to the big man. Giddings's head disappeared under the water and popped up again. He managed to hold onto the rope, and Marty started to pull him closer. Seconds later, Giddings's hands were grabbing the ladder. Marty knew he had twenty more seconds to save his own life. "Get him!" Simon screamed as more of his men appeared along a catwalk above him. Below, Marty grabbed a piece of rebar and slashed holes in two of the Zodiac rafts. As the air whooshed out, he dove back into the water. At the same exact moment, bullets rained down all around him and pinged the platform.

More men appeared beside Simon, guns drawn. They aimed their weapons at the spot where Marty had disappeared and fired.

But Marty was already gone.

Simon looked down at Giddings, who was still unconscious. Then he looked to his men, who just stood there. "What are you waiting for?!" He screamed, and the men charged down the steel stairs to the rafts. One by one, they jumped into the first three rafts. They sank under them immediately, thanks to Marty's handy rebar-work, leaving them dog paddling in the frothy waters, trapped under the platform.

Simon looked at Giddings, who lay there bleeding, his eyes shut. The guy was dying, and he knew too much. No one was watching; they were all busy trying to catch Marty. Simon made up his mind and moved quickly. He bent down, and his eyes met Giddings', who stared at him in horror. Simon looked away and pushed him over the edge and into the water.

Marty popped his head up for air and watched Simon's men struggling in the waters under the rig, then turned and continued swimming just below the surface. When he was far enough away from the rig he surfaced and floated on his back to rest, taking long, even breaths as he frog-kicked in the direction of the large coral reef a few hundred yards ahead.

The air tasted brackish, laced with crude, like there was a long line of sixteen-wheelers burning diesel in the air. The spill was worse than he thought. If it engulfed the reef, it would be all over for the coral in the area. All life depended on it and that included the fishermen from the Isle of Good Fortune, the remote island that was nestled about four miles east.

The people on the island had been living off the sea and the reef for centuries. The oil spill was about to threaten their way of life – and they didn't even know that a man-made disaster was looming over their heads like a tsunami.

I need to warn them, Marty thought.

He heard shouting in the distance behind him, coming from the platform. They'll be coming after him again. He had a good head start, but they would catch him before he could make his way to shore.

He swam with all his might toward the dim lights of the shoreline, which could only be the Isle of Good Fortune.

That was when he heard the tinkle of a bell. He recognized the sound immediately. It was a power-line bell, used by fishermen to alert them that they had hooked something. He looked up and saw a small fishing skiff anchored in the reef, lapping quietly against the calm waters of dawn.

There was something on the skiff sticking out over the bow, and even in the moonlit silhouette, Marty could see it was his surfboard.

There was also noise. A noise that didn't fit out here on the reef. He thought he could be wrong, but he was pretty sure he knew what it was.

Someone was snoring.

CHAPTER 4

Actually, *two* someones were snoring, like two rappers, off beat, and off key. One voice was high-pitched and the other hoarse. Marty, dead tired, beaten, and swimming for his life, laughed out loud. It had been a horrible night so far, and it felt good to just let it all out.

He aimed for the fishing skiff, drifting against an anchor chain of shiny steel, and he swam with great purpose. The snoring grew louder the closer he got. When he got to the starboard side of the aged wooden vessel, he grabbed it with both hands and pulled himself up far enough to peer over the gunwale into the boat and immediately discovered the source of the snoring: an ancient man.

He was fast asleep under a tarp with only his head exposed. He had wrinkles on his wrinkles, and long white hair. Marty was annoyed to see the old man sleeping on his surfboard, but relieved to find it unharmed. There was one other thing. The source of the other melodic snoring. It came from a boy, about Marty's age, his head sticking out of the tarp a few feet away, his right hand gripping a large fishing net that was unfurled over the side. The other gripped the side of the boat. In his sleep. Gripping with enough force to bend steel, it seemed to Marty.

Marty jerked his gaze in the direction of the distant oil platform and squinting, he could just make out the fast-moving watercraft, illuminated between ocean swells and lit from behind by *The Black Hole*. He quietly blew out a frustrated breath. He had hoped they had given up on him.

First came the lemon-yellow chevrons of light from the onboard spotlights, panning and crisscrossing the choppy waters looking for him. Then came a Zodiac and the silhouettes of two armed men.

The gray light of dawn was pushing the night away. Soon the morning mist would evaporate, and they'd spot him from afar and hunt him down. He knew he didn't have enough time to reach the island.

He looked again at the old man and the boy sleeping in the boat, which was rocked idly by the waves, and quickly worked his way down the side of the boat to the stern, away from them. With arms raised, he slid like an eel, going face first under the tarp. In the process, he tore his shirt sleeve as he sneaked into the belly of the boat and vanished from view. Once under the tarp, he pressed against the port side wall, trying not to breathe or make a sound. He felt safe, but he couldn't stay idle. He had to send his auto-location data to Gabby again before it was too late.

He hesitated before he wrote: They tried to kill me. On the run.

On the other side of the tarp, the old fisherman had awakened and heard whatever it was stirring underneath the tarp. His name was Francisco Mateo Alejandro de Souza, *a mouthful if you said all the names together,* but you didn't have to because those who knew him, whether they loved him or hated him, called him Cisco.

The boy, Lucas, opened his eyes and looked in dismay, pulled from a sweet dream. He was about to say something when Cisco put a finger to his lips to keep him silent, and Lucas obeyed.

Cisco grabbed the tarp in both hands and ripped it back, revealing Marty underneath, lying in a weird position.

Marty breathed hard and just stared at the old man. When their eyes met, he knew he was safe.

"I wouldn't have thought the way he's lying there was humanly possible!" Cisco said to Lucas in Portuguese, and Lucas got up, looked at Marty, and burst out laughing.

"D-do you speak English?" Marty asked, panicky.

"I don't blame you for being frightened," Lucas said to Marty in English. "Cisco has a very scary face." He laughed again and Marty chuckled.

He got up on one elbow, looked around, and saw the Zodiac heading their way.

"Hey, uh—" Marty said, pointing in the direction of the oncoming Zodiac.

"Please don't let them know I'm here!" He said. "If they find me, they're going to kill me!"

The man and the boy looked and saw what was coming. The Zodiac's loud engine split the quiet dawn.

"This one is a bad one," Cisco said, recognizing the man standing in the Zodiac even from this distance. Moving down the boat, close to Marty, Cisco grabbed Marty's shirt where it was ripped, and tore the sleeve off.

"Hey! What are you doing?!" Marty yelled.

The old man's face was close to his, and Marty stared in his eyes, which shone in the dark like fireflies.

"Saving your life," Cisco said, and whipped out a switchblade knife, opened it with a whoosh, grabbed Marty's wrist and sliced his forearm about where the sleeve was, drawing blood.

"Are you nuts?!" Marty yelled and tried to pull away, but Cisco had a firm grip on him. He could have broken the hold but the way the old man held him told him he knew a few martial arts tricks too. "I know that hold," Marty said.

"Good," Cisco replied. "Then hold still. I'm almost done." He sopped up some blood with the shirt sleeve, then let Marty go.

The raft drew close, and their wake rocked the skiff.

"Put some pressure on that cut and get down *now!*" Cisco whispered. "I'll handle this."

Marty realized the man was trying to help and ducked down under the tarp, disappearing from view.

Cisco and Lucas pretended to sleep.

Marty watched with one-eye peeking out from his hiding place. There were two men in the Zodiac: Jorgito, the big one with salt-and-pepper gray hair, and Carlos, the small one with a clean-shaven head. They were low level security guards on the rig and Marty wondered why Simon sent them, of all people. Probably because he trusted them to get rid of Marty away from the prying eyes of too many people on the rig. Jorgito cut the engine. The Zodiac's wake rocked Cisco's skiff again. Cisco and Lucas pretended to wake up.

"Yo, Cisco!" Jorgito yelled. They knew the old man.

Cisco opened one grumbling eye and scowled. "What do you want?" It was obvious Cisco didn't like him.

"We are looking for a boy," Jorgito said. "Americano. A bit taller than that one," he said, pointing at Lucas.

"What have you been drinking, Jorgito? It's just me and Lucas out here," Cisco chuckled.

Jorgito grabbed his rifle and jammed the barrel at Marty's surfboard. "What do you call that?"

"In the land of human beings, it is called a surfboard," Cisco shot back.

Under the tarp, Marty slunk deeper into the hold.

Carlos gave Cisco a suspicious look. "You sure you didn't see a boy surfing out here?"

"I heard shots," Cisco said. "Then I found this." He picked up Marty's torn, bloody shirt sleeve and waved it like a checkered flag at the man, then tossed it to Carlos. He didn't like him either.

Carlos, disgusted by the wet blood, shoved it at Jorgito, who angrily snatched it.

"Where'd you get this?" Jorgito asked, raising one eyebrow.

"I pulled it out of the water," Cisco said calmly. "Your poor guy was swimming away and met these hungry things here." He took his lantern and hung it over the side, lighting up the water below where a school of sharks were circling forty feet below. "If I were you, I wouldn't try anything crazy," Cisco said. "I think they're still hungry."

The men were unnerved. "Y-yeah but, what do we tell the boss?" Carlos asked Jorgito.

"Tell him he got eaten by sharks," Cisco replied, pulling his pistol from under the tarp, getting the drop on them. "Now get out of my waters, you've done enough damage with that spill of yours."

Jorgito chuckled and shook his head. "Come on, Cisco, we both know that thing ain't loaded."

Cisco pointed his pistol skyward and shot at the moon with a loud thunderclap.

Startled, the men laughed. "Okay, okay, take it easy, we get the point," Jorgito said.

Under the tarp, Marty held his breath.

Cisco stood up in his boat, spreading his bony legs for balance, never taking his eyes off Simon's men. "Poor kid. Who is he, by the way?"

"The boss' stepbrother," Carlos said.

Cisco didn't show his feelings, but Lucas looked shaken.

"I'm keeping the board," Cisco said.

Jorgito shrugged. "It's all in the family," he said, laughing. "We'll tell the boss the sharks did our job for us." Both men laughed. Jorgito fired up the engine, spun the raft around and took off back to the oil rig.

When the Zodiac was a comfortable distance away, Cisco ripped back the tarp, revealing Marty underneath.

Marty managed a smile. "Thank you for saving my life."

Cisco chuckled. "I hate these lowlifes. Know how to row?"

"Do I know how to row," Marty said, as if he were the world's best rower. "I'm a surfer. I paddle. Same thing, right?"

"Why is your stepbrother trying to kill you?" Lucas asked.

Marty scratched his head, trying to figure out what to say, when a loud braying sound like a hundred voices cut through the sounds of the reef:

"HAWWWW-HEEEE-HAWWWW!"

"What was that?!" Marty was happy to change the subject.

"Penguins," Cisco said.

"What are they doing down here? Don't they live in Patagonia?"

"They are tourists on vacation," Lucas said. They like the weather here."

"And the sandy beaches." Cisco said.

"And the food." It was Lucas' turn again. "Speaking of food, I'm hungry, boss," he turned to Cisco, who pulled out two bananas from a cooler and handed them one each. The boys wolfed them down.

"Thank you," Marty said. I know I'm putting you in danger. I'll find a way outta here as soon as possible. I promise."

Cisco shrugged. "I smell trouble. Lots of it," he said.

"Where are we heading?" Marty asked.

"My home, Ghost Beach, on the most western point of the Island," the old man said, motioning towards the island. "Why, are you thinking of forwarding your mail there?"

Lucas and Cisco laughed.

"I don't want to put you in danger," Marty said.

"I think you've already done that," Cisco said. "And I think we share the same enemy."

He motioned in the direction of the rig. Lucas nodded in agreement.

"Thank you," Marty said, swept with emotion. For the first time since his stepbrother tried to kill him, he felt safe.

Cisco turned the motor on and aimed the boat eastward.

"Let's go home," he said.

CHAPTER 5

A thousand Magellanic Penguins brayed as one as they glided past the reef just offshore from the Isle of Good Fortune.

All the penguins but one.

This particular penguin was slower than the rest because one of his flippers was smaller than the other. It wasn't a huge difference, just enough to slow him down. He was used to it. He had made the swim three times in three years: once as an offspring, once alone as an adult, and this time, the third time, with his mate. She swam up ahead and they communicated with a special call they had between them.

The penguin raft made the trip every winter. They swam from the Falklands up the coast of Argentina to the plentiful islands off the coast of Brazil.

They had been moving in a line over a mile long for three months, through many lights and darks for more than two thousand miles. They filled themselves with baby squid and fish along the way, and stored them in their bellies, undigested, to eat later. When they linked together to rest, they looked like a giant penguin blanket floating on the swells and currents.

For this penguin, his mate was everything. This was their first year together, and they had no offspring.

They were heading to the grassy shores further north where no humans roamed, and there was no danger of predator birds. A place where they could pass the time and mate before making the long journey back with the changing of the seasons.

The penguin let out his special call, a low, braying sound that only his mate could recognize. There was a faint reply in the distance, and he knew it was her.

He loved diving and enjoyed the local fish, the Jaraqui and Tabaqui. He dove below, down to where the water cooled off, where he spotted a squad of baby squid. He jetted through the water after them and when they sensed the pursuit, they billowed out clouds of black ink. He exploded through the ink and gained on the squid, but just as suddenly as they appeared, they veered to the right at an impossible angle and vanished among the sharp glassy spires of the offshore reef. The penguin stopped chasing and surfaced. The squid were gone, and there was nothing else to eat. No fish, no squid, barely any life at all. He was all alone. He could no longer hear his tribe. He called out to his mate again.

There was no answer. He had drifted off course. But by then, it was too late. In an instant, he was stuck, caught in the thick blackness he was supposed to swim around. Trapped in the stuff that smelled so bad it burned his nostrils, choked him, and would not let him move.

He was trapped in a blanket of sticky crude oil. The black gold which the humans on the oil rig drilled out of the bottom of the ocean. When refined, it would become a source of energy, flying airplanes, sailing boats and driving cars while making the planet hotter, polluting the air and threatening to destroy life on the planet.

The poor penguin wasn't aware of all that. He was stuck inside a trap and couldn't move. He cried out for help, hoping his mate would hear him. She was the only thing that mattered in his life. Now he was all by himself, alone in the darkness, stuck in a thick black goo, with no hope of survival. He cried out again. It was all he could do.

The morning didn't give him any hope either. He was weak and hungry and there wasn't much he could do to change his looming fate.

He was about to die.

CHAPTER 6

Two days earlier, Gabriela "Gabby" Ferrari stood a couple steps above the crowd at the famous Spanish Steps overlooking Piazza di Spagna in the city of Rome, Italy. It was early afternoon, and she scanned the audience at the square. She was addressing a crowd of about two hundred people, who showed up to a spontaneous rally she had organized earlier that morning.

Most of the people in the beautiful square couldn't care less about the small demonstration, but Gabby's heart was filled with gratitude for those who showed up on such short notice.

She was searching for final words when she heard the sirens wailing, and she knew that she didn't have much time. "I hear the police coming," she said into the loudspeaker she held in her hands. "This is a peaceful demonstration. Stay calm." The crowd cheered. Some people booed. "We know that they are not evil," she raised her voice. "They are just wrong!"

A few people chanted her name: *Gabby! Gabby!*

She slid her phone into her sock. She always carried an extra phone with no SIM card in her pocket as a decoy.

Five police cars entered the square with flashing lights. She raced down the stairs and wove herself through the parting horde.

Two dozen police officers marched in, led by a tall captain. From the corner of her eye, she spotted the police chief himself with his arms crossed. It was unusual to see him at such a small event, as it was below his pay grade. She had known him since she was a child; he was an old friend of her father's, and she referred to him as Uncle Tony. Though he stood at a distance, he kept a watchful eye as the captain ran the show.

"I'd like to say good evening to the Roma police," she said into the loudspeaker while marching towards them. "Thank you for joining the fight to save our planet."

The crowd roared with laughter.

Someone threw a firecracker into the air. In quick succession, more firecrackers were thrown, filling the square with explosions. Gabby knew that the police would take this as a sign to move in and crush the demonstration. They pushed and shoved people, waving their batons in the air. People yelled in fear and anger. The tall captain yelled into a bullhorn advising everyone to leave the square immediately. Gabby yelled back into her bullhorn: "This is a peaceful demonstration! You can't do this to us! It's against the law!"

"We *are* the law!" the captain shot back. "And this is an unlawful assembly. Everyone - go home. Now!"

Someone threw an egg, and it smashed against the captain's face, the yellow yolk running from his forehead down to his cheeks. Gabby heard the collective gasp. The captain looked unfazed. He wiped his face with a handkerchief. About two dozen protesters clashed with the police. The others left the square or looked for a place to hide. Someone detonated a smoke grenade that filled the air with choking fumes. Gabby stood in the middle of the square yelling, "Stop it! Stop the violence! Stop the beating!" but things were already out of control. Someone got close to her and handed her a gas mask. She didn't see who it was. Her eyes welled with tears and her lungs ached as she quickly pulled it on. She wanted to thank the mysterious stranger, but he had already disappeared into the fog of white smoke. She took a few steps forward when something hard hit her on the back. She fell flat on the cobblestones, her bullhorn skittering away from her.

"Gabriela Ferrari, you are under arrest!" The voice was muffled. She was lying flat on her stomach and handcuffed. All she saw were shiny boots approaching. Without looking, she knew it was the captain.

The captain continued, "Gabby, you are a great disappointment to us, especially to your family. It's a shame my next call will be to your father to let him know his daughter is in jail on at least five charges."

Gabby didn't answer. Her father knew the drill and, although he wasn't happy about his only daughter's activism, he realized that he couldn't do much to dissuade her. This wouldn't be her first time being arrested.

Ten minutes later, she was tossed into a holding cell in the central police station about two blocks from the Coliseum. She sat on a wooden bench. They'd already confiscated her fake mobile, and she knew that she couldn't use the phone that was hidden in her sock because there were hidden cameras everywhere. She was about to ask for a bathroom break when the cell door opened, and a policewoman came in and told her to follow her.

"Where to?" Gabby asked.

"What? And spoil the surprise? You'll find out soon enough," the policewoman answered with a smile.

What is wrong with them? Gabby thought. They were treating her much too nicely this time around, from the moment the police car raced her back to the station to when they uncuffed her and a police physician checked her oxygen level. She was fine. The mask had protected her, but she thought about the ones who weren't so lucky. It made her sick.

At the end of the corridor, the police officer showed her a door.

"They are waiting for you," she said.

Puzzled, she opened the door. It was a windowless conference room. She saw Uncle

Tony. He nodded, flashing a smile. Two men in suits sat at the other side of a long table.

"Please sit down, Gabby," the chief said. "I'm sorry we had to arrest you. but we didn't have time for a better plan. Once we explain, I know you'll understand."

She sat down, unsure where this conversation was headed.

"First, Chief, I'd like to know why you sent your policemen to shut down a perfectly harmless demonstration," Gabby demanded.

"We had to do it, Gabby," the chief said. "I'd like to introduce you to these two gentlemen; both are from the AISI. Mr. Conte and Mr. Ranieri."

She looked at the two men and knew those weren't their real names. The AISI was the Internal Information and Security Agency of Italy.

The man who went by the name Conte said, "Ms. Ferrari, we had credible intelligence that a terrorist organization known as The

Chamber, planned on kidnapping you. We had to act to protect you."

Gabby gasped. She'd gotten a lot of threats recently from haters around the world. But a terrorist organization! Kidnapping! It all seemed unreal.

"When?"

"Today, at your demonstration," Uncle Tony said. He looked worried, something she'd never seen before. "Fortunately, we were able to spoil their plans."

"They called the police complaining about a fight your people allegedly started at the Piazza Di Spagna, but our people were already there monitoring the situation," said Ranieri. "We played along. They planned to abduct you while the police clashed with your team. That's why we had to get you out of there first."

Gabby was relieved but not impressed. "Great. I suppose I should thank you then."

"For your safety, our people will be protecting you twenty-four seven," Conte said.

"Thanks again but there's no need, really," Gabby said. "Uncle Tony, could I use the bathroom please?" She sounded desperate.

He nodded. She was surprised that the policewoman wasn't waiting for her outside. She entered the bathroom and went into one of the stalls. She opened her phone and saw a ton of messages waiting for her. Nothing stood out. She went back to the conference room.

"I think it's better for me to just disappear for a week or two," she told the three gentlemen who waited for her. "I'll be in a safe place while you find the people who were behind the plot to kidnap me."

"Where?" the chief asked.

"I'm not sure," she lied.

"You can't go to Brazil," Mr. Conte said firmly. They had hacked her phones and knew where she was heading. She tried hard not to explode.

"Are you bugging me?" she demanded. She gave them a stern look, waiting for them to lie to her.

"We had to," Mr. Conte said apologetically. "In order to protect you."

"Thank you," she said. "Now, if you don't mind, I want you out of my life. I can take care of myself," She turned to Uncle Tony. "Am I free to go?" He nodded, and before they could respond, she stormed out of the room.

It was another rehearsal day for the world-renowned conductor, Maestro Carlo Ferrari, Gabby's dad, at the Parco Della Musica. He stood at the podium, his arms outstretched, baton in hand, ready to point to the concertmaster to hit the first note when his assistant came rushing across the ancient floorboards to the podium and whispered in his ear. He gave her a look, then nodded and sighed. He turned to the orchestra, defeated. "Carry on. I'll be back soon."

"Take your time, sir," the concertmaster told him. He had watched a TikTok video - one of many featuring Gabby's arrest - so he correctly guessed what the maestro had to deal with.

The maestro smiled gloomily. "Okay," he said. "Don't wait for me. When you're done, take the rest of the day off." The musicians clapped and began playing as he walked out.

He jogged to his office when his phone vibrated.

"Hello Tony," the Maestro said. "I hear you have Gabby. Again. Maybe it's time you started charging her rent."

"Not quite," the police chief said, chuckling. "She was sitting here next to me half an hour ago but unfortunately she took off without a proper goodbye."

The news reeled the maestro.

"You don't know where she is?" he asked.

"She went directly to the airport and boarded a plane to Prague," the chief said.

"Prague?" The Maestro choked. "Why?"

"Don't worry, our people are waiting for her there. She is safe."

The chief said he'd come by later to the Maestro's villa and explain.

The call ended. The Maestro entered his office, and he was floored by what he saw.

"Hi, papa," Gabby said in a cheerful voice. "It's SOOO good to see you!"

"I thought you were long gone," her father said, pretending to be calm.

"Not yet," she said. "But I need your help. And you have to swear you won't tell anyone."

CHAPTER 7

Cisco navigated his skiff towards the island, avoiding the oil slick. He was worried the tides would spread the oil to the island shores.

He sighed.

"I can barely hear the penguins now," Marty said.

"They're moving on," Cisco said.

"Don't they stop on the island?" Marty asked, surprised.

Lucas chuckled and shook his head.

"'Fraid not," Cisco said. "Each year they swim past us. Thousands of them. For generations."

"Wow," Marty said.

"But they never stop here," Lucas shrugged. "Ever." Thinking about it made him sad. "Wish they did. It'd make us a sanctuary."

"So where *do* they stop?"

"They land where it's safe. Where there are no predators," Cisco said.

"What kind of predators do you have on your island? Jaguars? Birds? Do the Skua come this far North?

"No Skua," Cisco said with a shrug. "Just us. Humans."

Marty nodded. "Yeah, I guess you're right. Mankind is hardly a peaceful animal. Just ask my stepbrother."

Cisco shut off the engine. He and Lucas grabbed the oars and started rowing in the other direction.

"Where are we going?" Marty asked.

"Gotta check my net," Cisco said. "That's why we came out here in the first place. Make sure it doesn't get ruined by the slick." He and Lucas rowed carefully into the fog.

"Your slick stinks!" Lucas yelled, pointing his finger at Marty, who balked at first. He was right though. The air smelled so bad they could hardly breathe. As they moved through the fog, the air grew cooler, and the smell dissipated. Cisco stopped rowing and declared, "This is it," as he reached over the side to pull up a large green glass ball expertly sewn into an old net. He examined it with relief and announced, "The slick didn't get it. Let's pull it in."

Lucas got up, came over, and he and Marty pulled in the net, hand-over-hand, while Cisco examined it and rolled it up into the boat. In ten minutes the last of the net was neatly stowed in the boat. "And not a bit of that gooey stuff!" Cisco said. "No fish either. But it looks like I'll live to fish another day. Let's head back," he turned to Marty. "Don't worry, kid, I'll make sure no one finds you. Do you mind rowing?"

"It would be an honor," Marty said, and took the oars from Cisco.

"*hawwwwwwww...*"

It was a penguin bray. Not distant. Just weak. Marty heard it first.

He looked at Cisco, who nodded. "Yeah, I heard it too. I'm not deaf yet," he said. "But I'm afraid it's too late for that one."

Marty felt a pinch of nerves in his stomach. He closed his eyes, centered himself, and prepared to row. Just then, the boat rocked from underneath, knocking him off his seat and onto his back. One of the oars slipped into the water. He lunged after it. That was when he looked down into the water and saw what was rocking the boat.

They were surrounded by sharks.

CHAPTER 8

They had to get the oar. Marty held on to Cisco's waistband and the old man stretched out over the gunwale. He grabbed the oar in the water just as one of the sharks bit down on the other end and swam with it, pulling Cisco overboard.

Marty threw down the other oar and dove into the water after Cisco. Lucas dove in too. The two grabbed him by the scruff of his pants and lifted him over the side of the skiff, saving him. Lucas hauled himself back aboard just as one of the sharks rammed into Marty's thigh underwater and bit down. He screamed in agony. Cisco, dripping water, looked back in horror. "Quick!" he shouted as he and Lucas stretched out their hands. Marty reached up with both of his and Cisco and Lucas dragged him back into the boat in one rapid move, just as another shark snapped its jaws shut behind him, missing him. "Get the kit!" Cisco said, pointing to the red fishing tackle box in the bow, then turned to Marty and rolled him over.

"Where'd he get you?"

"Thigh," Marty said, gritting his teeth.

Lucas hurried over with the first aid kit and pulled open the rusty lid with a creak.

Cisco yanked his belt out of its loops around his waist, rolled Marty over, and wrapped the belt around Marty's bloody leg above the thigh. He tightened it into a tourniquet using his fishing knife as a lever.

"Not too bad," Cisco said. "One-inch gash. Looks like he nicked ya."

"Thanks," Marty managed to get out between clenched teeth. The pain was excruciating. He tried not to cry out. "You-you saved my life," he mumbled. He was feeling faint.

"That's the second time tonight the sharks went after you," Lucas smiled, still shaken.

"But this time they didn't kill me," Marty forced a smile.

"Yeah, well, now we can all stop worrying about sharks," Lucas said.

"How do you figure?" Marty asked.

"The odds of getting bitten by a shark are two million to one. The odds of getting bitten if you *know* someone who got bitten, go up to twenty million to one," Lucas said.

"You made that up - didn't you?" Marty mumbled. He tried not to scream. The pain was unbearable.

"Yea," Lucas admitted with a grin.

Marty knew that if he laughed, it would hurt. He was sweating profusely. Cisco snapped his fingers at Lucas. "Get me a hook and some line. It's only an inch, but I'm going to sew it up."

Five minutes later, Cisco bit off the end of the gut line, having stitched up the gash and splashed some salt water on it. Then he wrapped a long strip of bandage and a piece of cloth around the wound. "That'll do it until we get to land," he said, then looked around. "Looks like we drifted off-course in all the excitement. He turned to Marty. "How's your thigh feel?"

"Stings like hell," Marty replied.

"Chew some of these," Cisco said, and snatched an old brown bottle of Anacin aspirin from the red box and tossed it to him. "Give him some water from the canteen after he chews them down," he said to Lucas. "It'll work faster that way. And keep moving it so it doesn't stiffen up."

Marty looked warily at the bottle of aspirin, then opened it and dumped two in the palm of his hand. He looked at Cisco, then to

Lucas, then downed the pills, following with a few swigs of water from the old canteen.

"Thanks," Marty said.

"*Hawwwww-heeee-hawwwwww...*"

"That wasn't me, was it?" Marty quipped, and Lucas chuckled then looked at Cisco.

"It's that penguin again. Guess I was wrong about his demise," Cisco said.

"The rest of the raft must have moved on," Lucas said, "and left him behind. We should do something."

The old man wasn't having it. "We're going home, where we can all get some rest. It's been a long night, especially for you," Cisco said, jerking his thumb at Marty.

Haaaawwwwww...

"Please, let's get him to safety," Marty said. He felt weak and tired, but he didn't want that penguin to suffer, not if they could do something.

Lucas looked at Cisco. "Can't argue with that," he said. Without another word, Lucas grabbed the oars and rowed in the direction of the cries until the penguin came into view.

"He's alive," Cisco said. "But I'm not sure he'll live much longer, even if we save him."

"But we gotta try," Marty said, and Lucas agreed.

"Okay," Cisco said. "Let's give it a shot."

CHAPTER 9

The Ryanair flight from Rome to Prague landed at 9:30 PM. A woman by the name of Gabby Ferrari took a taxi from the airport to an apartment in the center of town. Before she settled in, she heard a knock on the door. Two plainclothes detectives from the local police showed her their credentials and asked her to join them at the local police station. An hour later, Uncle Tony got a message from Prague that the woman they picked up wasn't the Gabby Ferrari he was looking for. They just had the same name.

Uncle Tony realized that Gabby had fooled him and the AISI. And now she was gone. And he had no idea where she went. He was on his way to Gabby's dad's villa, and he knew that Carlo would be upset.

While people in Rome were looking for Gabby, she was on a flight headed to Sao Paulo, Brazil. She wore a blond wig and used a fake passport, one of a dozen she often used. This other Gabby Ferrari, who flew on short notice to Prague, was one of her supporters with the same name who was happy to help Gabby disappear into thin air. In Sao Paulo she was met at the airport by one of her local supporters, a guy named Vini. He drove her into a little apartment on the outskirts of town where she planned to stay out of sight before her appearance at the summit. She settled in the car and opened her phone. Marty's message popped onto the screen.

Hi Gabby. On the run. They tried to kill me.

Then she read the earlier message.

I figure you're not far away. I discovered an intentional oil spill at United Petroleum's Black Hole oil rig. They locked me up. I might be in danger. Marty.

Her heart was racing. "Vini, have you heard about a United Petroleum oil rig called the Black Hole?

He nodded. "Yea, it's about a couple hours' boat ride from the city."

"Can you get me there?" she asked.

"When?" he asked, his gaze fixed on the rearview mirror, making sure no one was trailing them.

"Now," she said.

If he was surprised, he was very good at disguising it.

Sixteen-year-old James Lee, AKA Kaboom, took a sip from his Diet Coke. He had been playing *Call of Duty* for the last nine hours, but he wasn't alone. About fifty thousand fans watched him play. It was noon in Seoul, Korea and Kaboom was playing because he loved it—and the money he made wasn't bad either. He was one of Gabby's most enthusiastic supporters, and when she needed his other talents as a skillful hacker, he made himself available.

Call me. It's urgent. G.

He told his viewers that he was taking a short break. He was Gabby's eyes and ears on the internet. Monitoring risks. Looking for bad people who were plotting to hurt her and their cause. He did a lot of defensive work and from time to time went on the offensive. There was a war raging behind the scenes between climate activists like Gabby and people who thought that global warming was a hoax and tried their best to sabotage the activists' work.

"Hi Kaboom, I hope I'm not interpreting something important," Gabby said.

"I'm fine. I see you are in Sao Paulo," he said cheerfully.

"I am," she said. "Just landed. I need a favor."

"I'm all ears," he said.

She asked him to look into the Black Hole. While she was talking, he was already working his magic. Kaboom was a genius in breaking into locked vaults of information and finding hidden secrets. It made him feel great exposing the most evil plots the worst people on the planet were concocting in the dark. He was more than happy to go inside United Petroleum's communication network. He hated oil barons.

"I got something," he said after about three minutes. "They were looking for a kid named Marty. Supposedly he was killed by sharks when he tried to flee."

It hit Gabby like a ton of bricks. "Are you sure?" she screamed.

"This is the chatter I'm getting."

"I'm texting him. Wait."

"Are you OK? Where are you?"

Seconds later she got his message.

"I'm on a boat, on the way to Ghost Beach, Isle of Good Fortune."

"Are you safe?"

"Yea. But my brother is out to kill me."

"I'm on my way," she wrote back.

"Thanks," Marty *wrote.*

"Did you see our chat?" she asked Kaboom.

"Yes."

"Keep an eye on him," she asked. "And get me the coordinates of this beach."

"I am," he said.

"You're the best," Gabby said.

He smiled. *He was the best.* Then she said "There's one more thing. I'd like you to hack the Italian security service."

"I've never hacked into a security service," he said. "Exciting!"

She laughed. "I knew there was nothing in the world that could scare you," she said. "I want to know everything they have about an organization called The Chamber."

He thought for a second. "Okie doke, I'm on it."

He let his fingertips dance on the keyboard. He loved this so much.

They arrived at Sao Paulo harbor, Port of Santos and boarded a speedboat. The captain greeted them. He looked like someone who had been awakened abruptly not so long ago, but he didn't complain. He was one of *them*. Gabby sat at the back, and Viny and the captain were at the wheel, all wearing life vests. The engine roared to life, and they were on their way minutes later.

CHAPTER 10

A minute later, Kaboom called her again. He sounded irritated. "I'm hitting a wall," he admitted. "Do you have any leads? Anything?"

Gabby knew she might be crossing the line, but she had to take the chance. "I'm sending you my uncle Tony's phone number. He's the chief of police in Rome and a family friend. I believe you'll find leads on his phone regarding the people working on the Chamber's case. Their names are Conte and Ranieri."

Kaboom got to work while they were talking. It surprisingly proved easy to hack into Uncle Tony's phone. Within ten minutes, he had also hacked into Ranieri and Conte's phones without having to breach the agency's systems. It became apparent that one of the agents, Conte, was involved with the group that had attempted to kidnap Gabby. To make matters worse, the kidnappers were tracking Gabby's phone. Kaboom traced them back and hacked into their network.

He reached out to Gabby on one of her burner phones. "I'm sorry, Gabby," he said. "What happened?" she asked, alarmed. "They were able to trace your conversations with your friend, Marty, on your main phone," Kaboom said. "And they know where you are and where you're heading."

"The people who tried to kidnap me?"

"Yes."

"Bummer," she said. She had taken great care to change phones and discard SIM cards, but she had been reckless this time around.

"The good news is that I'm inside their network," he said, pleased.

"Great!" she said, still feeling guilty. "What should I do with my phone?"

"Keep it active," Kaboom said. "I can scramble your conversations and texts. I don't want them to suspect that you know they're eavesdropping."

She let out a sigh of relief. "Thank you," she said, and he disconnected without another word.

Two hours later, she could spot the glistening lights of the Black Hole in the distance. Soon, she caught a whiff of the odor emanating from the slick. The captain veered south and went around the slick to approach Ghost Beach. She could see the deserted shore through the morning mist. When the water became shallow, the captain turned off the engine and informed her that they couldn't proceed any further.

"We can walk through the water," Vini suggested. "It's shallow."

"I can go alone," Gabby said. She retrieved shorts from her backpack and changed into them. "Thank you guys. You are great!" she said and hugged them.

Slipping the backpack over her shoulder, she climbed over the boat's railing and descended into the ocean. The cool water reached her knees. Waving a final goodbye, she walked slowly towards the beach.

CHAPTER 11

The penguin was badly trapped in the slick.

"Big one," Lucas said. "Half-alive."

"A male," Cisco said.

"How can you tell?" Marty asked.

"Males are bigger than females," Cisco said. "You see enough of them, you learn how to tell the difference. He knows he's in trouble."

They studied the poor creature trapped in the ooze of spilled oil.

"Have you ever seen one stuck like that?" Lucas asked.

"Only once," Cisco said, worried. "And it was already dead."

Marty's eyes widened. He could already see that the poor creature could not move.

"He's going to die if we don't get him out," Cisco said, and rowed with all his might.

The penguin was engulfed in the slick and the more he struggled, the less he moved. He tried crying out for his mate, but he could barely make a sound now.

The skiff slowly approached the trapped penguin. It was indeed a Magellanic Penguin with all the markings, now soaked and covered in this poisonous ooze. The creature opened his blackened beak, but no sound came out.

Cisco grabbed his red first aid box, snatched out a pair of latext gloves, and pulled them on, turning to Lucas. "Hold on to my belt and when I tell you — pull," he said, and moved the skiff a little closer to the trapped creature. "Can you do it?"

"I'll do it," Marty said.

Cisco looked at him. The kid was just bitten by a shark, but he pulled himself together.

"Are you sure?" he asked.

Marty nodded enthusiastically. Cisco got on his knees at the gunwale. "Ready?"

Lucas grabbed the back of Cisco's belt with both hands and started to slide forward. Marty got behind Lucas and wrapped his arms around his waist.

Cisco reached over the gunwale to where the penguin was trapped, took hold of it with both hands, and leaned back. "Now!" he shouted, and Marty and Lucas pulled with all their might.

The penguin came away from the thick crud with a loud *slurp*, braying loudly.

"Take it easy, penguin," Cisco said gently, placing the creature in the wooden tub where he usually kept his bait. The penguin was so covered in oil there was very little left of his tuxedo white visible, nor of the two telltale bands.

"Put some gloves on!" Cisco ordered Marty and Lucas, and they pulled on a couple pairs from the first aid box. "Now hold him tight," he said to Lucas.

Lucas nodded and grabbed it with both gloved hands and held fast. He had never touched a penguin before. Never even seen one this close.

Cisco took a bucket, scooped it into the sea and poured the sea water into the tub as the penguin struggled in Lucas' hands, terrified. Lucas held the bird with gentle hands and the penguin finally calmed down after a few moments. Cisco squirted a bottle of blue dishwashing liquid at it and began the slow process of cleaning the poor creature. Once he got the penguin's head fairly clean and the bird could breathe normally again and move his neck around, he scooped out the dirty water and added more clean water.

"Sorry penguin, gotta do this for your own good," he said, and dropped a cover over the tub, sealing the penguin inside. He turned to Marty and Lucas. "He can breathe now, so we'll get the rest of him cleaned up when we get home."

The penguin's bray echoed under the metal cover of the wash tub, and the cover lifted up and moved a little as the penguin struggled underneath.

"Better sit on it!" Cisco said to Lucas, "so he doesn't hurt himself."

Lucas jumped on the cover and bounced around as the penguin seemed to regain some strength and tried to escape again. Cisco leaned back in the boat. "We won't use the engine; it might spook him." He observed Marty and asked, "Marty can you row? How's the pain?'

"I'm good," Marty said, and grabbed the oars, wincing. His thigh hurt like nothing he'd ever felt before, but the aspirin was starting to kick in.

"We'll hit home in a couple of hours," the old man said.

Marty started rowing.

After a few minutes, the rhythm of the motion of the boat relaxed the penguin, whose brays turned to coos, and he never made another sound the rest of the way back to the beach. In fact, he was so quiet, Cisco had Lucas check under the lid a couple of times to make sure the bird was still breathing.

He was fine.

An hour passed and then they heard the faint sound of an engine. Cisco listened intently. "I hope it's not trouble," he said.

"I'm expecting someone," Marty said. His eyes shone.

"Who?" Lucas asked.

"Help," Marty said.

Cisco and Lucas exchanged looks.

"Don't worry," Marty said. "Trust me."

Suddenly, the faint line of the shore emerged through the night's mist.

"Welcome to Ghost Beach," Cisco said. "The place I call home."

Marty saw a deserted shore with a few palm trees. He was tired and his wound was burning and itching. There was nothing inviting on the deserted beach.

Cisco and Lucas jumped off the skiff into the shallow water and pushed the skiff to the sand. Marty stood up and joined them gingerly.

Cisco uncovered the tub. The penguin sat calmly and didn't budge.

"He's the first penguin to come to the island since—," Cisco said, thinking about it. "Since *forever*!"

Marty and Lucas lifted the tub out of the boat and set it on the sand. The penguin didn't move inside.

"Let's open it inside the house," Cisco said. "Otherwise, he'll run away."

Lucas lifted the lid, and the Penguin popped his head outside. He brayed anxiously.

Marty saw a deserted shack. It stood on a small hill overlooking the ocean.

"Nice, ah?" Lucas asked proudly. "It's Cisco's."

"Yea," Marty said. "There must be other people on the island."

Lucas nodded. "They live two miles down south, in the village."

"So why does he lives here alone?"

"Some people prefer to be by themselves," Lucas said. "Me included."

They climbed the hill towards the shack. "I bet you are hungry," Lucas said.

"I am," Marty said.

"Good," Cisco said, overhearing the conversation, "I'll put some tea on and warm up the moqueca."

Marty knew that moqueca was a traditional Brazilian fish stew, but he never had it before.

"It's really good," Lucas said, licking his lips. "The other day I ate the entire pot, and it made Cisco angry. He said I was selfish."

"You are," Cisco said, and for a second, he seemed angry.

"I'm a shellfish," Lucas winked.

"Not funny," Cisco scowled.

"He made me clean the shack and do the dishes," Lucas said, turning to the old man, "So we are even."

"Anyway - I cooked another pot," Cisco said. He was very hungry himself.

They approached the door. "Welcome to my humble home," Cisco announced. "Please come in." There were no locks. As he opened the door, a strange, soapy scent wafted towards him, mingling with the aroma of the almost-empty fish stew pot on the table. A girl he didn't know was sleeping there, her head resting on the table.

He couldn't believe his eyes. *Am I dreaming?* he wondered, as Marty came into the room and stopped in his tracks:

"Gabby!" Marty exclaimed.

She opened her eyes and smiled.

"Hey Marty," she said.

CHAPTER 12

As the sky turned from black to blue, about a mile further away, a man lay face-down, spread-eagled on the beach. He didn't move. The tide was in and lapped at his bare feet.

A young kid was the first to spot him. He ran to the village and told his mom what he saw. She walked to the village grocery store and told the owner, who was also the mayor about the man on the beach. Minutes later, Santos—the mayor—and three other men approached the man warily. He was a giant of a man, and his face was buried in the sand. It took the four of them to roll his body over.

He looked dead. No doubt about it. His pants were torn, his United Petroleum company shirt was ripped to shreds, and he was covered in cuts and dried blood.

Santos checked the man's pockets for identification. He knew for sure that the man must have worked on the oil rig. As Santos reached into the dead man's pocket, the man's eyes snapped open. The man grabbed Santos by the shirt, pulled his face close, and grinned, blood trickling from the side of his twisted mouth. "Can I help you?" he cackled.

Santos screamed in horror.

The man screamed back.

The twisted grin was the most frightening thing Santos had ever seen, and he was sure he was seeing a monster.

"It's the devil himself!" he screamed again. He felt the man's grip on his throat tighten like a screw. He couldn't breathe. His eyes bulged. He watched his comrades run for their lives, leaving him to die.

The monster suddenly oozed blood, fell forward on the sand, and rolled over onto his back. Santos breathed heavily. He released himself from the man's grip and stood up, shaken.

Now it was Santos' turn to run for his life.

Behind him, Giddings looked up at the clear blue sky. He wasn't sure if he was dead or alive. Was he dreaming? He closed his eyes again and passed out. He stayed there for hours, waking up several times as the morning made way for the day. Slowly, the memories of last night came back to him.

Was it the damn boy, Marty, who pushed him into the water again? No. Marty had saved him. But someone had pushed him back in. But who? He tried to remember.

He stood up slowly and began to walk.

It was then that he saw a deserted shack on top of the hill overlooking the beach. *I must be hallucinating*, he thought, when someone broke out of the shack and started running towards him. It was a penguin.

And then he saw the boy himself, Marty, running after the penguin.

But no, this is not happening, he thought, before passing out, dazed and confused, on the hot sand.

End of Book 1

READ BOOK 2 FIRST CHAPTER!

CHAPTER 1

The giant of a man woke up with a start and found himself surrounded by leaves. Everything itched while a thousand ants crawled all over him. Disgusted, he shook them off. His clothes were torn and spotted with dried blood. Two monkeys watched from a nearby tree.

He was lying on the ground, in a jungle. He remembered dreaming of walking on a beach. There was a boy, chasing a penguin. The boy was familiar, but he couldn't recall his name.

He heard water running nearby, so he stood up slowly and found a stream and a small waterfall. He was so thirsty, he gulped in the cool water from the stream. He wondered how he had ended up here, and as he looked at the logo on his shirt, UP - United Petroleum, the memories started flooding in.

His name was John Giddings, and he used to work as the head of security at United Petroleum's oil rig, the Black Hole, off the shores of Sao Paulo, Brazil. So, how did he end up in the middle of a rainforest? The monkeys chattered, seeming to ask the same question.

He remembered that the boy's name was Marty, and Marty had saved his life. But did he really see him on the beach chasing a penguin? As he tried to figure things out, he noticed that the two monkeys were eating fruits from a nearby Cupuaçu tree. He felt hungry yet the fruits were too high for him to reach. Suddenly, one of the monkeys threw one at him, then another, and another. Giddings picked up one of the fruits from the ground, opened it with trembling hands, and savored the sweet pulp. It tasted like ice cream.

As he ate, everything came back to him. He used to be a heartless killer in the service of others. But now, he found himself in the middle of nowhere, eating fruits given to him by monkeys, and tears of gratitude welled up.

The monkeys screeched and darted away, and Giddings sensed something was wrong. He scanned his surroundings and caught sight of the piercing green eyes of a jaguar, just fifty feet away. Frozen in fear, Giddings felt as though the entire jungle had gone silent. But to his relief, the jaguar simply turned and disappeared into the foliage. After waiting for a few tense moments, Giddings turned and sprinted in the opposite direction.

Made in the USA
Las Vegas, NV
28 July 2023

75345477R00060